For Cheryl—
Keep being the bright light you've always been.

Quill Tree Books is an imprint of HarperCollins Publishers.
Bring Up the Sun
Copyright © 2025 by Derek Anderson
All rights reserved. Manufactured in Capriate San Gervasio, Italy.
No part of this book may be used or reproduced in any manner whatsoever without written permission except in the case of brief quotations embodied in critical articles and reviews. For information address HarperCollins Children's Books, a division of HarperCollins Publishers, 195 Broadway, New York, NY 10007.
www.harpercollinschildrens.com
Library of Congress Cataloging-in-Publication Data
Names: Anderson, Derek, 1969–2024, author, illustrator.
Title: Bring up the sun / by Derek Anderson.
Description: First edition. | New York : Quill Tree Books, an Imprint of HarperCollins Publishers, 2025. | Audience: Ages 4–8. | Audience: Grades K–1. | Summary: After inheriting sun-shining duties from his grandfather, a young sun learns to trust himself and shine brightly, no matter what others may say.
Identifiers: LCCN 2024005397 | ISBN 9780062402608 (hardcover)
Subjects: CYAC: Sun—Fiction. | Self-confidence—Fiction. | LCGFT: Picture books.
Classification: LCC PZ7.A53313 Br 2025 | DDC [E]—dc23
LC record available at https://lccn.loc.gov/2024005397

The artist used ink and Photoshop to create the digital illustrations for this book.
Typography by Rachel Zegar
25 26 27 28 29   RTLO   10 9 8 7 6 5 4 3 2 1
First Edition

Bring UP the SUN

By Derek Anderson

Quill Tree Books
An Imprint of HarperCollinsPublishers

Sun was very small when his grandfather decided to retire.

And his father was busy with other projects.

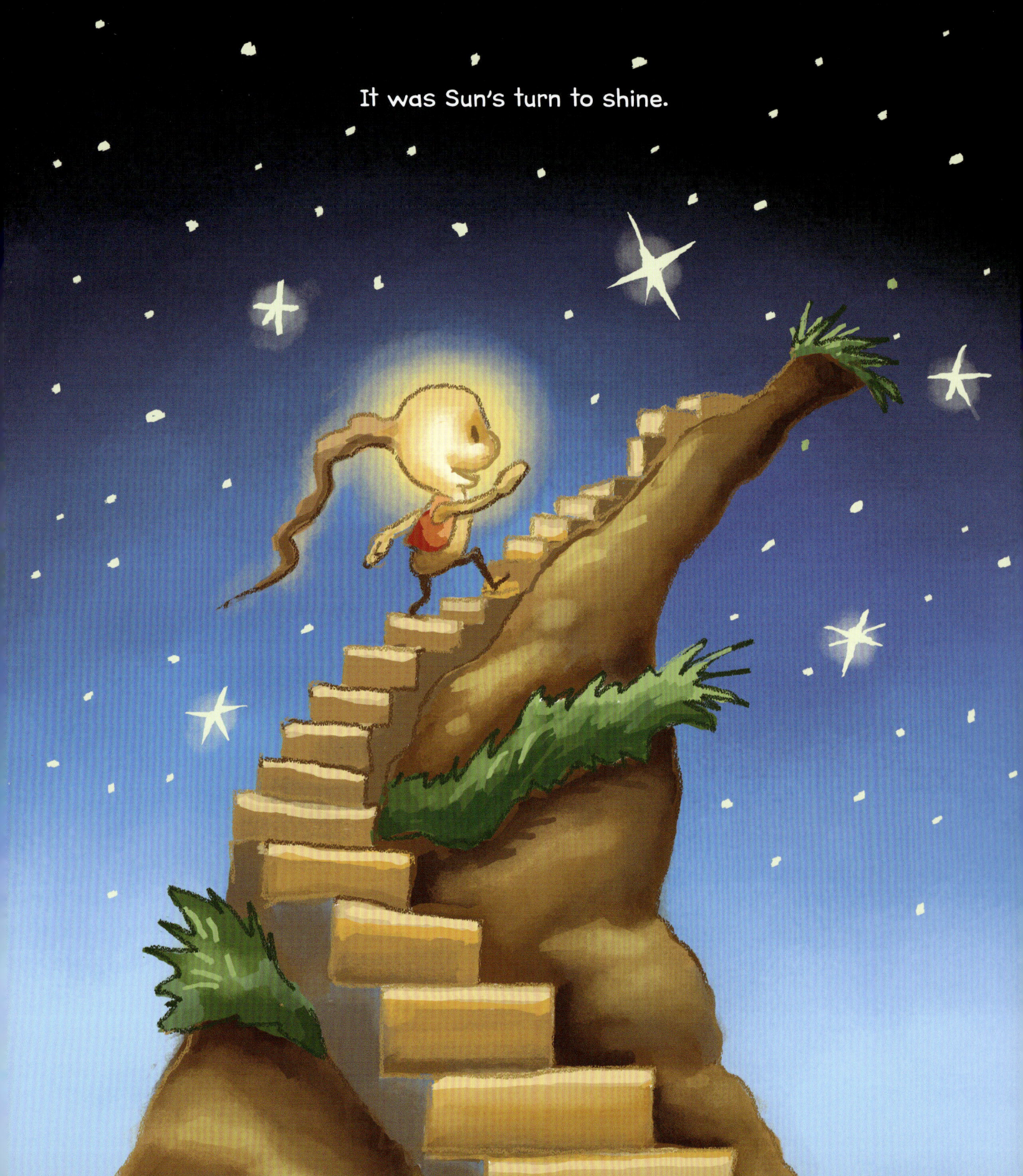

He wasn't big and bold like his grandfather.
But he tried his best.

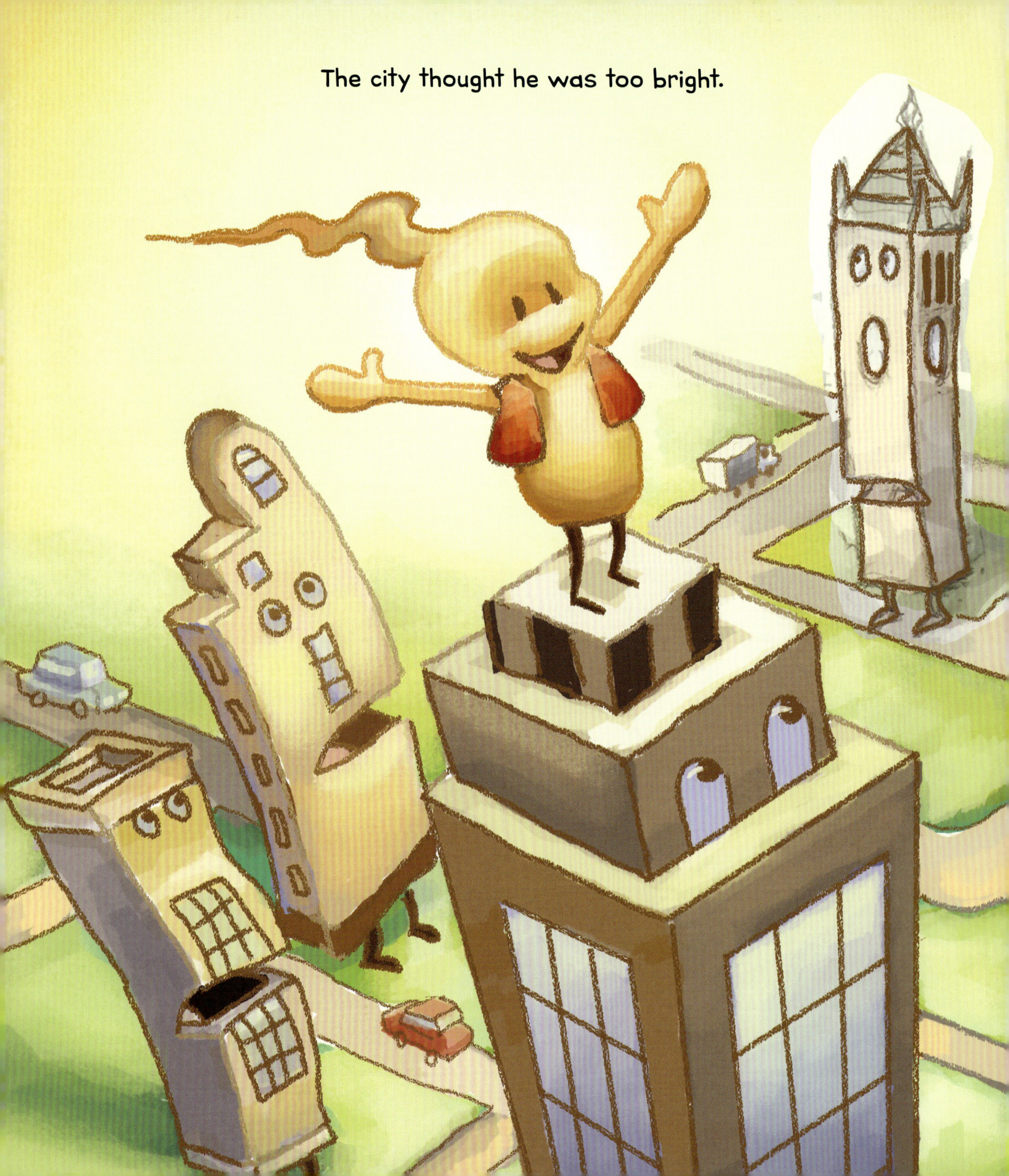
The city thought he was too bright.

Sun gave up.

What was the point of shining if nobody liked his light?

That night, while the clouds, the mountains, the trees, and the city slept, Sun went off to visit his grandfather.

The next morning, Sun was still on his way back from visiting his grandfather, so he didn't bring light to the world.

He filled the forest with light and shined on every cloud in the sky, turning them brilliant shades of yellow, pink, and purple.

Sun spread his joyful light everywhere
and shined . . . anyway.